THE KNIGHT OF SPURS AND SPIRITS

TERRY DEARY'S KNIGHTS' TALES

THE KNIGHT OF SPURS AND SPIRITS

Illustrated by Helen Flook

A & C Black • London

First published 2009 by
A & C Black
an imprint of Bloomsbury Publishing Plc
50 Bedford Square, London WC1B 3DP

www.bloomsbury.com

Text copyright © 2009 Terry Deary
Illustrations copyright © 2009 Helen Flook

ISBN 978-1-4081-0620-4

A CIP catalogue for this book is available from the British Library.

This book is produced using paper that is made from wood grown in
managed, sustainable forests. It is natural, renewable and recyclable.
The logging and manufacturing processes conform to the
environmental regulations of the country of origin.

Printed and Bound by CPI Group (UK) Ltd, Croydon CR0 4YY

3 5 7 9 10 8 6 4 2

Chapter One
Drafts
and Deer

England, 1609

The castle is grim. The castle is grey.
And the castle has a gruesome tale
to tell.

The castle is known as Hylton Castle and it stands – grim, grey and gruesome – on a hillside by the River Wear in the north of England. You can see it there today – a sad shell of a hollow hall.

The castle is cold. The roof is gone, but the sun never shines inside the grim, grey, gruesome walls.

But when the last knight lived there, the castle could be warm. When the fire was lit in the Great Hall, it was warm there by the fire. Tapestry curtains hung on the walls and kept out the draughts.

Chairs had cushions high and soft to keep out the draughts as you sat by the fire ... *if* you were one of the lucky ones that sat by the fire.

Lucky – like the last knight of Hylton, Sir Robert.

Logs as large as dogs flared in the fireplace and sparkled on the tapestry walls. Sir Robert took an iron poker and pushed it into the fire. Then he took a flagon of wine and emptied it into his silver cup.

When the poker was glowing red, he pushed the tip into his wine and watched it bubble and boil, spit and sizzle.

Sir Robert sat back in the chair and sipped the warm wine.

"Marvellous!" he smiled. It was a fat-faced, well-fed, red-cheeked smile.

Sir Robert stretched out a lazy hand and pulled on a rope that hung beside the fire. Somewhere in the castle halls, a bell jangled.

Moments later, the door opened and a girl hurried in. She was dressed in a fine, grey dress with a white, linen collar and an apron as white as snow.

Sir Robert, the last knight of Hylton, looked up. "Ah, Mary!"

"Yes, Sir Bobbert!" said the girl in a voice as dry as hay. Her throat went dry when she stood in the piggy-eyed gaze of her lord, and the words got jumbled in her mouth. "I mean ... Sir Robert, sir, sorry, sir."

"The weather, girl."

"Yes, sir," said Mary, and bent her knees in a low curtsey.

"Yes, sir *what*?" the knight rumbled.

"Yes, sir, whatever you say, Sir Bobbert ... Robbled ... Bobbit."

"I asked you about the weather. What's it like outside?" Sir Robert could have pushed open the shutters on the windows of the Great Hall, but he was too lazy for that.

"Sunny, sir," Mary panted, trying to remember.

"Sunny, eh? Marvellous!"

"And cloudy," she wittered.

"Uh? How can it be sunny if it's cloudy?"

"Sometimes it's sunny and sometimes it's cloudy. It changes. When a cloud crosses the sun, it stops being sunny and when..."

"Enough!" roared Sir Robert.

Mary trembled.

"Is ... it ... raining?" the last knight of Hylton asked slowly, as if he were talking to a slow and slightly stupid snail.

"Not today, Sir Bobble ... but it might rain next Tuesday, the wise woman of Wearside said in the market..."

"I ... do ... not ... want ... to ... know ... about next Tuesday!" he said. "If it is a fine day today, the deer will be out. Tell the Master of the Hunt I will go hunting this morning. Catch us a nice fat deer for dinner."

"Yes, sir," said Mary. She bobbed a curtsey and turned towards the door ... both at the same time. Her ankles became tangled, and she almost tripped over. "Ooopsy-daisy! Sorry, Sir Rubble!"

"And tell that useless stable boy ... Skeleton..."

"It's Skelton, sir. Roger Skelton."

"Whatever his name is ... tell Skeleton to have my bay mare ready, brushed and saddled."

"Yes, your lard-ship ... your lord-shap..."

"And take this wine away ... it tastes of burnt wood," said Sir Robert, passing the silver cup to the girl. "A quick nap and then I'll be ready to ride," he sighed. "Ma-a-a-a-rvelous!"

Chapter Two
Wine and
Warmth

Roger Skelton sat at the kitchen table. He supped at a bowl of broth that was hot from the pot that hung over the fire. His thin, round shoulders were covered in a thin, round jacket of green and his skinny hands trembled as he held the spoon. "I'm cold, so cold!" he murmured to himself.

The fire burned brightly and a whole pig hung on a spit over the flames. The spit had a wheel at one end, a wheel like the one on a watermill. Inside the wheel was a small, brown dog. The dog walked forward inside the wheel. As it walked, it turned the spit. As the spit turned, the pig turned over the fire.

The roast-pork smell filled the castle kitchens. The pig fat dripped into the fire and spluttered and spat and burned with a fierce flame.

The door crashed open and Mary the maid ran in.

"Oh, Roger, there you are. His lordship is going hunting in a while…"

"I'm cold!"

"He wants his best bay mare made ready," the girl went on.

"But I'm eating me dinner! I need it to warm me up. Didn't I tell you, I'm cold?" he whined. Roger was a whiner.

Mary placed the great goblet of wine in front of the boy.

"Sir Robert has just heated up this goblet of wine," she said. "Now it's wasted. Drink it and it may warm you up."

Roger wrapped his hands around
the silver cup and felt them glow.
"Ooooh! Warm."

"And it's warm *inside* if you sip it,"
Mary said. "Otherwise, I'll just have
to throw it away."

Roger put the silver goblet to his
lips and sipped. It was a mixture
of fine wine and ash from the poker.
It warmed his mouth, warmed his
throat, then warmed his gut. The
warmth began to spread over his
body. "Ahhhh!" he sighed. "Lovely."

The warm spirit of the wine went up Roger's nose and made him a little dizzy. "Ooooh-eeeeh!" he said, and wobbled. A silly smile spread over his face and his eyes closed. Slowly, slo-wly, s-l-o-w-l-y, s-l-o-o-w-l-e-e-e-ee, his face fell forwards onto the table.

"Poor Roger," Mary sighed. "It's good to see you happy and warm for once, but I can't let you sleep." She rested a hand on his shoulder and jiggled it. "Wake up."

The boy opened his bright eyes. "Hello, Mary!" he said. "I must have dropped off."

"Sir Robert wants you to saddle his bay mare."

"Does he?"

"Yes, I told you. He's going hunting. You'd better hurry. You know how he hates to be kept waiting, especially when he's off murdering little deer."

Roger rose to his feet and wobbled a little. "Ooooh! That soup's made me all giddy," he giggled. "I'll go and saddle that grey mare now."

"*Bay* mare," Mary moaned. "Get it *right*, Roger, for goodness' sake."

"Bay ... grey ... play ... day ... way ... hay!" Roger grinned and wobbled towards the door. He pulled it open.

"No, Roger!" Mary cried.

Roger walked through the door and slammed it behind him. There was a crashing and a clattering, like a knight in armour falling off his horse and into a bucket of nails.

Mary tore open the door and said, "Oh, Roger, that's the pan cupboard!"

"Ooooh!" said the boy, and wobbled towards the other door.

"Wait!" Mary sighed. Roger stood as still as he could. Mary walked across to him and pulled the saucepan off his head. "Now, Roger, off you go and saddle Sir Robert's *bay* mare."

Roger dragged his feet into the stableyard. The feet didn't seem to want to go where he wanted them to go. He stepped into the stable and saw the pile of hay in the corner, ready to feed the horses.

"I'm cold," he said, as he sat in the hay and pulled some over him to keep warm. "Sir Robert likes a little rest after his breakfast." Then he lay back in the tickly bed.

Roger's eyes closed...

The horses snorted. Roger snored.
A sparrow twittered in the rafters.
Peace fell on the stables of Hylton
Castle ... for a little while.

Chapter Three
Whip and
Wrath

Sir Robert, the last knight of
Hylton, woke from his nap. Hunting
horns were blaring outside his
window and that was what had
roused him.

He opened the shutters and saw
a grey sky as dull as the water in
the castle pond.

"The girl said it was a sunny day,"
he growled. "I must remember to
give her a thrashing when I get
back."

He stamped across the room and bellowed like a bull for his servants. "My riding boots! Where are my riding boots?"

When a boot boy ran along the passage with the big, brown boots, the lord roared, "And I hope they're clean. One speck of mud and you'll be thrashed."

"Clean as a raindrop, Sir Robert," the boy said proudly.

"Marvellous!" the last knight of Hylton chuckled, as he pulled them on. "And my spurs – fetch me my best silver spurs!"

A groom of the chamber brought in the shining spurs, a heavy, green cloak and a riding hat with a pheasant feather stuck in the side. "Your riding clothes, sire," the man bowed and bobbed.

"Marvellous! Now I am ready to go!" said Sir Robert.

The groom of the chamber gave a slippery smile. "Haven't we forgotten something?" he asked in a teasing voice.

Sir Robert hated that. He hated it when servants were smart and smug. He kept his temper. "I *have* forgotten something ... I was just seeing if you remembered, George."

"Geoffrey."

"What?"

"My name is Geoffrey, sire!"

"Whatever your name is ... you have forgotten something," the knight said sharply.

The servant brought his right hand from behind his back. "I don't think so. Here it is!"

Sir Robert looked at the stick with the large, silver knob on the top. "My hunting whip. Ah ... yes ... of course!" he said, snatching it from the slippery servant's slimy hand. "You've passed the test, George. Well done!"

"Thank you, sire," the servant bowed.

"Marvellous! Now," the knight said, as he marched through the hall and threw open the front gate, "I'm ready to go. Lead on, huntsman!"

The huntsman stood by a pair of grey deerhounds. "I think you have forgotten something, sire," he said.

"I think not! I have my boots, my cape, my hat *and* my whip. What more do I need?" shouted Sir Robert. "What more? Eh? Tell me!"

The huntsman coughed into his hand. "Ahem ... your horse, sire, your horse!"

Sir Robert turned redder than a robin's chest. "Yes! Yes! I know *that*! I know. No need to tell me..." He looked around wildly. "I ... I told that Mary girl to tell the Skeleton boy to bring it round to the front door, didn't I?"

Mary the maid was standing at
the kitchen door, just along from the
main gate. She turned pale.

"Oh, no, Sir Blobber! You just said
get it beddy ... I mean ret it geddy!
I mean..."

Lord Hylton hated to look a fool.
He strode toward the maid and
raised his whip. "First ... *first* you
tell me it's a sunny day..."

"It was when the sun set this morning ... I mean when the rose shine sunned this..."

"And then ... *then* you failed to tell Skeleton to fetch my horse!"

"Skelton, Roger Skelton, sir..."

"And now ... *now*!" he said, and raised the whip. "Now you call me a liar!"

The whip came down. Mary raised her hands to her head and turned away. The whip caught her across the shoulders and made her sob.

"I will go and ask Skeleton myself," the knight raged. "I will ask him if he was told to bring the horse to the main gate. I am a knight! I don't walk around getting my own horses, do I?" he asked and raised the whip again.

"Please, sir, no, sir!" Mary cried and scuttled back into the doorway.

The whip came down and missed her fleeing form. It hit the doorpost and made Sir Robert madder ... madder than a wasp with toothache.

"Someone will pay for this!" the knight screamed, and the ravens on the castle roof rose into the air in panic. "I'll kill Skeleton the skiver!" he roared.

Sir Robert Hylton marched off to the stables.

Chapter Four
Straw and
Sneezes

Roger Skelton was dreaming of eating a warm pie in a warm bed. As he was about to eat it, the pie was snatched from him by a skeleton...

"Skeleton!" came the loud voice. Roger knew that voice. "Skeleton!"

Roger stirred in the hay and slowly woke up.

Sir Robert Hylton was looking over the stable door at his bay mare. "Not saddled! Not even brushed!" he shouted. Wait till I get my hands on the boy ... Skeleton!"

Roger slipped deeper under the hay and tried not to breathe. But a sneaky seed of hay slipped up his nose. "Atch..." Roger almost choked as he tried not to sneeze. "Atch..." His nose tickled till his eyes wept. "Tchooooo!"

The hay blew away and Roger Skelton looked up at his master. "Good morning, Sir Robert," he said with a simple smile on his simple face. But it simply wasn't enough.

Sir Robert's face had been red
with rage. When he saw the stable
boy, it wasn't red any longer. It was
purple as a ripe turnip. But his voice
was soft. "My horse is not ready,
Skeleton."

"Lame, Sir Robert. You can't ride
her today. I was just coming to tell
you."

The knight stood over the boy and let his riding whip swing loosely by his side. "What's wrong with the mare?"

"Loose shoe."

"Let me tell you what I am going to do, Skeleton. First I am going to beat you for lying to me. Then I am going to beat you for not having my horse ready. That sounds fair, doesn't it?"

"Yes, sir... No, sir!" Roger cried.

In the castle kitchens, the servants heard the screams and covered their ears to shut out the sound.

Then the knight did a stupid and evil thing. He turned the whip around so he was holding the tip, then he struck the stable boy with the large, silver knob on the handle.

Roger had just turned to see why his master had stopped, so he caught the blow on the side of his head. If there had been a light in his eyes, it went out like a candle in a storm. He fell to the floor. Lifeless.

Sir Robert panted. "That will teach you, Skeleton. Now don't think a beating means you've been let off your duties. I still want that horse saddled, eh, Skeleton?"

Roger Skelton would not be saddling any more horses.

Sir Robert lowered the whip and spoke in a quiet, friendly voice. "Come on, Skeleton ... you've taken the punishment, now let's forget about it and carry on, eh?"

Roger Skelton would not be carrying on any more.

The purple face of the knight turned pale. He grasped the boy's thin, green jacket and pulled him up. Roger hung limp as wet washing on a line.

"It's all right, boy, I forgive you," said Sir Robert. "Skeleton? You can't be dead ... no, you can't! I hardly touched you." The knight's face turned red again. "How *dare* you die

... you ... you ... miserable little worm! This sort of thing causes so much trouble!"

The knight dropped the whip in the straw and carried the stable boy to the door. No one was in sight. Sir Robert looked out at the horse pond. He picked up a couple of old horseshoes and slipped them into the pockets of the boy's green jacket. Then he carried the little body to the pond and threw it out into the deepest part.

The knight wiped his hands on his hunting jerkin, then marched back to the castle, silver spurs jangling on the cobbles, to where the huntsmen were waiting.

"Hunt's off today," he said. "Horse is lame – lost a shoe."

Mary the maid peered around the door. "Where's Roger, Sir Pobble?"

"Eh? Oh ... ran off ... thought I was going to punish him because the horse lost a shoe! Ha! Simple boy. I wouldn't touch him. No ... ran off. That's the last we'll see of him!"

But Sir Robert Hylton was wrong...

Chapter Five
Heaven
and Hell

Mary missed Roger. She went to the stables to see if he'd come home. She looked at the bay mare. All its shoes were nailed on tight. As she turned to go, a glint of silver caught the setting sun. Sir Robert's whip lay in the hay. She picked it up. The silver head was wet and red with blood.

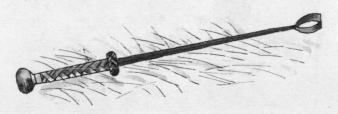

"Ohhhh, Roger!" Mary moaned. "What has he done with you?"

She searched the stable and barns and found nothing.

But two weeks later, Geoffrey the groom walked into the kitchen and sat at the table, shaking.

"What's wrong?" Mary asked.

"I was out walking Sir Robert's hounds today when I saw something floating in the horse pond. Some of the farm workers pulled it out. It was ... it was Roger's body."

Mary sobbed softly. "So that's what he did with him."

"Who?"

"Sir Robert," Mary said.

Geoffrey shook his head. "Lord Durham is here for dinner. Lord Durham is a judge for the county. There's going to be a trial in the Great Hall ... he says we can't have people thinking Sir Robert is to blame!"

"But he *is* to blame!" Mary cried. "The killer must be found and punished or Roger's spirit can never rest! Is the trial on now?"

Geoffrey nodded, and Mary raced along to the Great Hall. Sir Robert was sitting next to his friend, Lord Durham, and they ate slices of beef and bread from large plates in front of them.

Lord Durham munched and muttered, "How do you plead, Hylton?"

"Not guilty, my old fruit," Sir Robert replied.

"You didn't kill him, Bob?"

"Of course not, old bean."

Mary cried out in a clear voice, forgetting her fear. "He did! He said 'I'll kill Skeleton the skiver', and his lordship's whip handle was covered in blood."

Lord Durham glared at her angrily. "Silence in court!" He turned back to Sir Robert. "How did the blood get on the whip handle?"

The knight laughed and washed down his beef with a cup of ale. "Glad you asked me that. The lad, what's his name..."

"Skeleton?" Lord Durham said, looking at a scrap of paper.

"Skeleton," Sir Robert Hylton agreed. "He was asleep, so I gave him a little tap on the old noddle to wake him up. Must have had a thin skull, poor little chap. Died. Never felt a thing."

"They heard the screams down in the kitchens," Mary argued.

"Shut up," Lord Durham snapped.

"But..."

"Silence in court," the judge ordered.

52

"So how did Roger's body end up in the horse pond?" Mary said, bolder than she'd ever been.

Lord Durham turned to the knight. "I'm sure you can tell us that, Hylton, my friend?"

Sir Robert nodded his head sadly. "I tried to carry him to a doctor. But I slipped and dropped him ... just as I was passing the pond."

"Oh dear!" Lord Durham sighed. "I hope you didn't hurt yourself."

"No, but I got my boots a bit muddy trying to fish him out. In the end, I gave up. I mean ... he was only a servant, after all."

The judge spread some mustard on a piece of beef before cramming it into his mouth. "Yes, only a servant. But your story sounds

good enough to me. I think ... pass
me the ale, Rob, my old mate ...
thanks ... I think I have to find you
not guilty of killing him."

"Marvellous!" Sir Robert laughed.

Mary stormed to the table and
slammed her fist down so hard that
the silver plates and cups rattled.
"You call that fair?"

Lord Durham and Sir Robert
Hylton look at one another.

"Yes," they answered together.

Hot tears were pouring down Mary the maid's grubby cheeks. "Poor Roger will never rest in his grave. He'll haunt you, mark my words!"

Lord Durham pushed a plate of pork to one side so he could lean across the table and breathe his stinking breath in her face.

"Haunt us, will he?" he sneered, and spat crumbs on to the tabletop. "Push off, girl, or your master will haunt *you* with his whip."

That afternoon, Mary placed
spring flowers on Roger Skelton's
grave. "I hope you're warm now ...
in Heaven!" she whispered.

But Roger *wasn't* warm and Roger
wasn't resting in peace. His spirit,
they say, returned to haunt the
castle.

And, at night, when Sir Robert Hylton tried to sleep – some spirit seemed to haunt him. It was the shadow of a boy in a green jacket, hugging himself and moaning, "I'm cold ... so cold!"

Long after Sir Robert Hylton had gone to his own grey grave, the spirit still wandered Hylton Castle. And maybe it still does...

Epilogue

Hylton Castle is now in the city of Sunderland, north-east England. It was built around 1405, by William de Hylton, to guard the crossing point on the River Wear, about half a mile to the south.

Two hundred years later, the castle was owned by Sir Robert Hylton, a man with a fierce temper and a cruel streak.

Roger Skelton was Sir Robert's stable lad at Hylton Castle. His job was to look after the horses and keep the stables clean. But

Roger, they say, could be a little lazy. He really annoyed Sir Robert.

On 3 July, 1609, Sir Robert lost his temper with Roger Skelton one last time. He was furious when young Roger was too slow in bringing his horse. What happened next? There are a few stories:

• one says he speared the boy with a hayfork;

• another says he drew his sword and sliced off his head;

• another says he cut Roger's leg with a hay scythe and the boy bled to death;

• another says he beat Roger with his riding stick and cracked his skull.

But all the stories agree that Sir Robert threw the body into the castle pond. The body was found and it was clearly a case of murder.

Roger Skelton *may* have fallen on the pitchfork and *may* have cut himself with the scythe ... though he would not have cut off his own head (probably). It is pretty certain that he *didn't* throw himself into the pond.

Sir Robert Hylton was charged with the boy's murder. But he said it was an accident and, in September 1609, he was set free.

That much of the story is probably true. But then a legend grew up that said Roger Skelton came back and haunted Hylton

Castle. He wandered around crying, "I'm *cauld*!" (Now "cauld" is a northern word that can mean "headless" or "hooded" or simply "cold".)

One story says Roger Skelton was buried and his ghostly spirit rested. He was never heard of again. Another story says the Cauld Lad of Hylton never rested – his killer was not punished, so Roger is doomed to walk the Earth for ever more. Some people say they've seen him in the ruins of Hylton Castle to this day. Others say they've seen strange lights high up in the castle, even though the top floors have now crumbled and gone.

What do *you* think?

TERRY DEARY'S
EGYPTIAN TALES

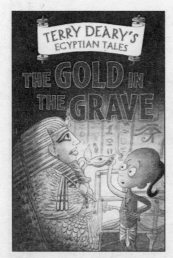

TERRY DEARY'S
EGYPTIAN TALES

THE GOLD IN THE GRAVE

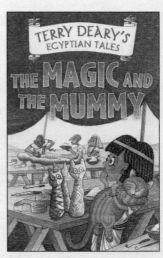

TERRY DEARY'S
EGYPTIAN TALES

THE MAGIC AND THE MUMMY

TERRY DEARY'S
EGYPTIAN TALES

THE PHANTOM AND THE FISHERMAN

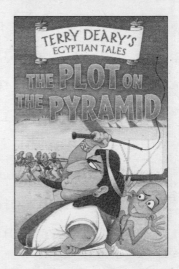

TERRY DEARY'S
EGYPTIAN TALES

THE PLOT ON THE PYRAMID

TERRY DEARY'S
GREEK TALES

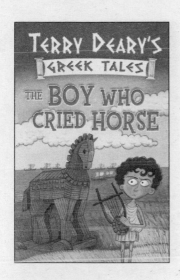

TERRY DEARY'S
GREEK TALES
THE **BOY WHO CRIED HORSE**

TERRY DEARY'S
GREEK TALES
THE **TORTOISE** AND THE **DARE**

TERRY DEARY'S
GREEK TALES
THE **LION'S SLAVE**

TERRY DEARY'S
GREEK TALES
THE **TOWN MOUSE** AND THE **SPARTAN HOUSE**

TERRY DEARY'S ROMAN TALES

THE GOOSE GUARDS

THE CAPTIVE CELT

THE FATAL FIRE

THE GRIM GHOST